ONE
MAGIC
BOX

ONE MAGIC BOX

BY ROGER AND MARIKO CHOUINARD

ILLUSTRATED BY ROGER CHOUINARD

DOUBLEDAY
NEW YORK   LONDON   TORONTO   SYDNEY   AUCKLAND

DESIGNED BY • DIANE STEVENSON / SNAP • HAUS GRAPHICS

Published by Doubleday, a division of

Bantam Doubleday Dell Publishing Group, Inc.,

666 Fifth Avenue, New York, New York 10103

Doubleday and the portrayal of an anchor with a dolphin

are trademarks of Doubleday, a division of

Bantam Doubleday Dell Publishing Group, Inc.

Library of Congress Cataloging-in-Publication Data

Chouinard. Roger.

    One magic box / by Roger and Mariko Chouinaird : illustrated by

    Roger Chouinard.—1st ed.

       p.   cm.

Summary: When one magic box falls from the sky, everyone is

puzzled, including the four policemen who come to inspect it, the

five big monsters who sit on it to see if it will hatch and the ten

flying saucers that hover over it to take a peek.

    [1. Counting.]   I. Chouinard, Mariko.   II. Title.

PZ7.C446370n   1989

[E]—dc19   89-1596

CIP

AC

ISBN 0-385-26203-5

ISBN 0-385-26204-3 (lib. bdg.)

ONE night, with no one in sight, a box fell
from the sky.

2

It was a very unusual box with TWO locks.

3 Out for a walk, THREE odd socks found the box.

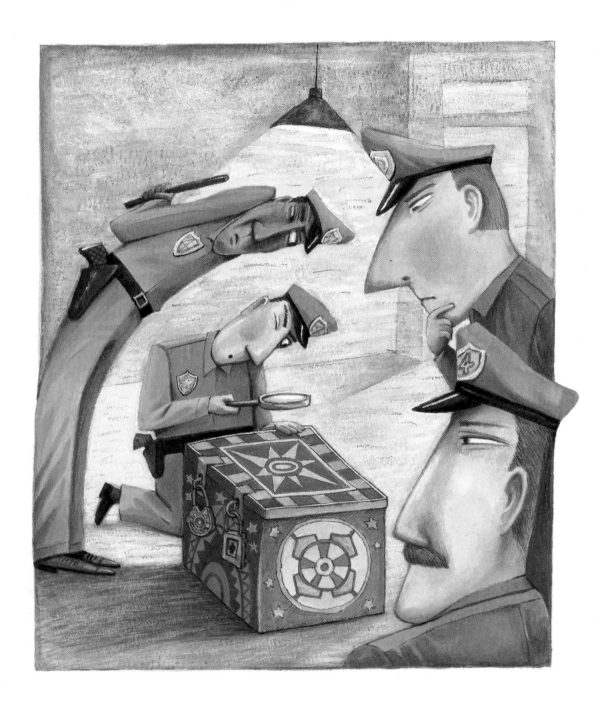

4 Soon, along came FOUR policemen, who inspected the box again and again.

5

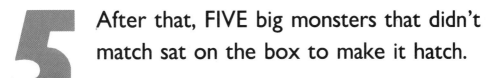

After that, FIVE big monsters that didn't match sat on the box to make it hatch.

6 Later, SIX keys came by and tried to unlock its locks.

7 Next, SEVEN lumberjacks lumbered up and attempted to saw the box in half.

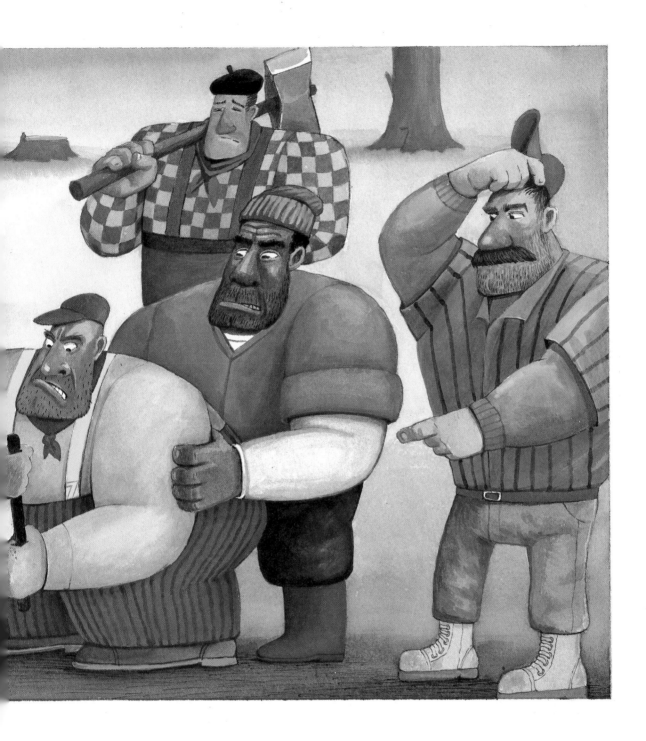

8

Then EIGHT feathers tickled the box and tried to make it laugh.

 Followed by NINE woodpeckers that attacked the box with their beaks . . .

10 TEN flying saucers that hovered over it for a peek . . .

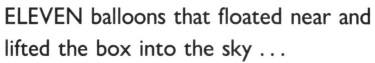 ELEVEN balloons that floated near and
lifted the box into the sky . . .

12 TWELVE butterflies that watched as it went gliding by.

13 Then the box sailed over THIRTEEN
fat acrobats . . .

14 and landed on a clown wearing FOURTEEN hats.

15

"My, my, fancy that," said a figure who suddenly appeared. "That's my missing magic box with the FIFTEEN magic stars and magic locks." And with a wave of his hand, the box opened on command.

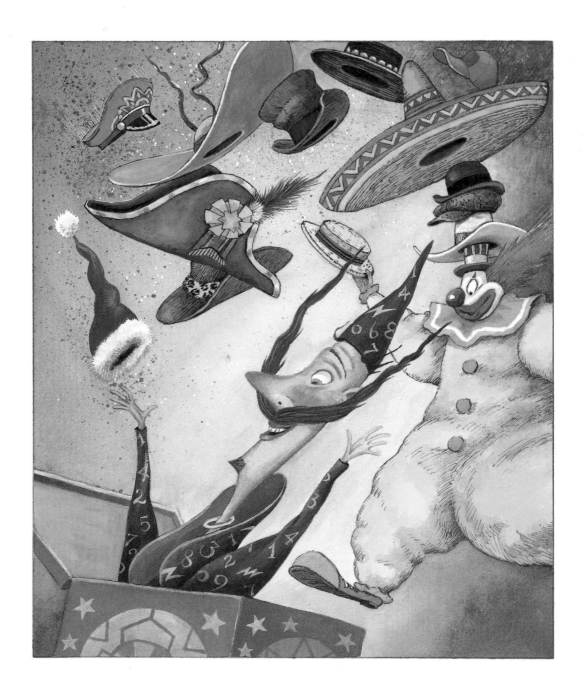

Then this thin figure, whose name was Count Magic, jumped in, followed by the clown with FOURTEEN hats . . .

plus THIRTEEN fat acrobats, and TWELVE butterflies, ELEVEN balloons, TEN flying saucers, NINE woodpeckers . . .

EIGHT feathers, SEVEN lumberjacks, SIX keys, FIVE
big monsters, FOUR policemen, THREE odd socks,
and TWO locks . . .

until all that was left was the ONE magic box.